Artemis
and the
Violin

Vanessa Chase

Artemis
and the
Violin

written by **Vanessa Chase**
illustrated by **Jo Gershman**

For permissions write:
Screech Owl Press
info@screechowlpress.com

Book & cover design by Jo Gershman.

First Edition: 2018

Summary: Accidentally trapped and transported across the country
from New Hampshire to Texas, a young chipmunk stumbles into
the adventure of a lifetime and a mystery that leads to unexpected
friendships on his quest to return home.

ISBN-13: 978-0692053096
ISBN-10: 0692053093

www.ScreechOwlPress.com

printed in the United States

For Kai, my little buddy

Table of Contents

Artemis
and the
Violin

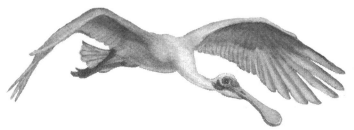

CHAPTER ONE

New Hampshire

"Artie, hold still! You're making it harder, you know," chirped Ellen. She reached into her straw basket and selected the next burr to poke into her brother's fur.

Artemis flinched and grumbled, "Well, you're supposed to be taking them out, not putting them in."

"No no, you look magnificent!"

"Take them out, Ellen!"

"Oh, Artie, you're such a worrywart."

"Ouch!" cried Artemis, as he felt another jab.

"There. *Very* fancy," she declared. His stripes were

now decorated with perfect lines of burrs. "Now I can call you Burrball instead of Furball. You'll look splendid for Papa's sing-along tonight."

"Take them out," he whined. "I want acorns. I'm hungry." He gazed longingly around the woods.

"Oh, Artie, let's have an acorn contest!"

"I don't want to stretch out my cheeks."

"Well, what's the point of being a chipmunk, then?

Come on. I can hold four and still whistle 'The Bear Went Over the Mountain.' You should try it." Ellen's ears twitched, and then she froze. "Wait!"

Artemis stopped breathing.

"Fox. Quick. Get in," she whispered as she tugged her brother into the entrance of her burrow.

Only then did Artemis notice the quiet crunch of leaves and the musky fox-fur scent. They waited in the hole while the predator skulked by.

"What would you do without me, Artie?" She patted her brother's paw fondly.

"I don't know. How do you always hear them? Take the burrs out. Please?"

"Okay, Artie. Fine. But then let's play hide-and-seek."

They cautiously climbed out of the hole. The fox had moved on.

As promised, Ellen plucked out each burr while she defined the boundaries for their game. "Not past the tall maple tree because there are people over there."

Artemis nodded impatiently. Chipmunks, by nature, never strayed far from home, so setting boundaries was just excessive.

"Okay, all out. I'll hide first," she said.

Artemis ducked back down into his sister's burrow, covered his eyes, and dutifully sang the usual two verses of "Fiddle De-Dee" as Ellen scampered off to hide.

"Fiddle de-dee, fiddle de-dee, the fly has married the bumblebee..." Artemis sped through the song.

Ellen had a good hiding spot. Artemis wandered through the woods, casually peeking inside holes and behind logs. He thought about where he could hide when it was his turn. He passed his own burrow. That would be a bad hiding spot. She would find him right away. Besides, he had spent far too long alone in there already. It had been a long, cold New Hampshire winter, and although spring was beginning, there were still patches of dirty snow on the ground. He hopped over the melting icy patches and was excited to see fresh green sprigs of grass poking through. When he reached the tall maple, he sniffed the mountain air. Instead of his sister's scent, he detected something far more tempting. Human food. It was starchy and heavenly, and he couldn't possibly resist.

"I'll just take a little break for a second," Artemis thought as he hopped into the humans' camp.

He sprang up onto a wooden picnic table to investigate. The scent was definitely coming from a large cardboard box on the table. The lid was open, but he couldn't see into it. He jumped right in. Crackers! He was thrilled. Most of them were locked in a closed jar within the box, but there were crumbs scattered everywhere. Artemis rummaged through the boring human supplies and collected the crumbs. He began to nibble. The crackers were salty and delicious. The more he ate, the more he wanted. Knowing he should get back to the game, he began stuffing his cheeks with crumbs to take back to Ellen. What a find it was! Ellen would reprimand him, but once she tasted them, she would understand.

Suddenly Artemis was jolted out of his reverie when a lid slammed down on the box. Everything went black. Artemis inhaled one ferocious gasp, choked on the crumbs, and then coughed them up. Panicked, he cringed in the corner of the box, listening.

From just outside, a woman's voice called, "Dale, we should get goin'! Can you put this stuff in the car? I'll get the tent."

Artemis felt his box being lifted and carried. Car doors slammed. He tried to push up on the lid, but it wouldn't move. Doors opened and slammed again, and then he heard the voices inside the car with him.

"Yuh mum just texted me," said the man. "Is yuh phone workin'?"

"Yeah, I gotta turn the ringer on. I'll text her in a sec when we're on the highway," replied the woman. "I just wanted to get packed up and on the road. Surprising what all fits in this little SUV. We almost coulda brought Champ."

"A drive like this? That dog would go nuts."

The engine started up. This was bad. Very bad. Horrified, Artemis realized that he would not be playing hide-and-seek, he would not be taking cracker crumbs to Ellen, and he would not be going to his papa's sing-along. The only party his family would have would be an endless search party.

CHAPTER TWO

Journey by Car

In the car the agonizing minutes stretched into hours. Artemis eventually lost track of how long it had been. He wondered how far a car could actually drive, and how long humans could sit in a vehicle. It was not something he had ever thought about. The car motored on and on, vibrating him to the bone. The motion was all wrong, and it made him ill. The dark box became too warm, and he sprawled out on the cardboard floor. His breath grew shallow as the temperature increased. He was overcome by sickness and then slipped into a distressed sleep.

When the box mercifully cooled, Artemis awoke and managed to chew through the cardboard. He squeezed through the hole, and found that it was also dark outside. It was a relief to breathe again. Up front, the humans were chatting about route numbers and exits, and they mentioned names like "Pennsylvania" and "West Virginia." Artemis quietly crept around the back of the car.

Eventually the vehicle stopped and the humans got out with one of the duffel bags. They were gone for the rest of the night, and Artemis slept curled up against a stuffed backpack.

In the morning the journey continued. On and on it went. Artemis was dizzy and sick again. He tried to find a cooler place to sit, but he didn't dare get too close to the humans. The front of the car did not smell right. The car got even hotter when they took "pit stops" and "McDonald's breaks," but Artemis never dared go up front and try to escape. When the front doors opened, the outside air was foreign and wrong as well. It frightened him. His only instinct was to hide. When the humans returned, the driving would continue. Hours stretched into days.

Through his nausea, Artemis could feel the sting of one remaining burr on his back, but he couldn't quite reach it. Grating, unnatural music with thumping bass lines blasted over the drone of the humans' voices. They used words like "oil derrick" and "Texas," but the conversations made no sense. He buried himself in the luggage and tried to tune everything out. With each stop, the heat got worse. It was impossible to think straight. In despair, Artemis climbed into yet another box, curled up, wept, and eventually passed out.

CHAPTER THREE
A New Land

Artemis awoke from his tormented sleep. The box smelled of sickness and musty fabric, but he was beyond moving.

"Oh, Ellen, I'm sorry. I shall die here," he whispered, wishing his sister was there.

With a start, Artemis realized that the car had just stopped. He struggled to regain consciousness. The humans were getting out. He crouched down farther in the folds of the canvas tarp and waited silently. There was a click and then a creak as the back door opened. Warm, humid air flooded in. Even under the fabric, the salty swamp scent made his nose crinkle in curiosity.

"Oh, my back," groaned the man. "Let's unload the stuff and find a good spot for the tent."

"Yeah," agreed the woman. "Aunt Kitty said her property goes out to the tree line, so anywhere back here is fine. The Smith Oaks Bird Sanctuary is super close."

The man grunted.

Boxes and bags were jostled, and then Artemis felt himself being lifted out of the car. His box hit the ground with a thud and a jangling as two metal stakes spilled out of the open top. He listened as more of the car was unloaded. Cautiously, he peeked out.

This was his chance. With what little strength he had left, he sprang from the box onto the dirt and scurried into the woods.

As he ran he heard the woman say, "Whoa! Was that a chipmunk?"

Catching his breath under a low tree limb, Artemis gaped at the land. It was definitely not New Hampshire. He was surrounded by prickly shrubs and great oak trees with stiff oval leaves and thick limbs that snaked around and dipped down to the ground. Gray-green moss hung like long fur from the branches around him.

Suddenly Artemis felt a terrible sting on his leg. Before he could think, there was another sting, and another. He twitched and jumped only to feel more fiery bites. Seeing a mass of tiny ants flooding around his feet, he darted away.

Artemis zigzagged frantically through the brush and up into one of the great trees. His legs stung and smarted. Dismayed, he crouched on a branch and licked his inflamed flesh. It was then that he realized how very hungry and thirsty he was. His last meal was the salty cracker crumbs that had tempted him into the box in the first place. That was days ago. Dizzy and weak, Artemis padded down the trunk of the tree and made his way into the woods.

He stopped to examine an odd acorn. As he stared at it, he had the uncomfortable feeling someone was looking at him. Even then, he was startled when an enormous squirrel dropped down right in front of him. Artemis stared at the creature, stunned. Her coloring was too rusty to be a gray squirrel, she was too massive to be a red squirrel, and she certainly wasn't a flying squirrel. The flying squirrels Artemis knew were dainty and nocturnal, and they had wing-like folds of skin between their legs. Nothing registered, and he stood, confused.

"Ah, hello," Artemis ventured.

The creature let out an aggressive "kuk-kuk-kuk" sound and hissed, "Get lost." She jerked upright, tail flicking violently over her shoulder. Her puffed-out belly was a foul, yellowish hue.

Artemis shrank back.

"And hey, you there!" she screamed.

Artemis cringed and then realized she was no longer talking to him. On a branch above stood a white and gray songbird with a black, mask-like stripe across his eyes. It was a shrike. The little bird was meticulously shoving what looked like a grasshopper onto a thorn. Impaled next to it were two more dried-up victims that Artemis did not recognize. Grunting softly, the bird finished his work and then began whistling cheerfully.

"Can you not put that there? Ugh, that's disgusting!" called the irritated squirrel.

"Now, now! No need for snootiness," chirped the shrike.

"Come on, I live in that tree! Now I've gotta look at your skewered meat every time I come home. Gross!" cried the squirrel.

"Well, don't look."

"How can I *not* look? Gross! I just can't *stop* looking!"

"Then go away," chirped the bird.

"They don't call you 'the butcher' for nothing. Ew, it smells. When are you going to eat those leathery lizards? Yuck! I just can't *not* look!"

"Yes, you can. Anyway, since when are you fox squirrels territorial?" The shrike resumed whistling without waiting for a response.

"And quit that whistling! It just seems so inappropriate," called the squirrel.

Artemis studied the carcasses lined up on the thorny branch. He wondered what the lizards looked like before. He'd never seen a lizard. Shrikes, yes, but definitely no lizards. And no fox squirrels.

Artemis jumped when the squirrel suddenly turned on him.

"Kuk-kuk-kuk!" This time she was not talking to the bird. She reared up on her back legs, and there was no mistaking the gesture. Artemis shrank and retreated in the opposite direction. The squirrel lunged at him but didn't follow.

Dejected, Artemis crept through the woods. The landscape soon changed as he headed south. The trees stopped, and there was open grassland. He weaved through the tall grass. A red-tailed hawk soared overhead, and Artemis crouched down until the bird had passed. It was difficult to see, but beyond the field the world appeared to stop. Curious, he hopped up onto a lone tree stump to get a better look. A road cut through the flat and bleak earth, and a single car approached and slowly disappeared westward. A black vulture glided by, but was uninterested in the living. Beyond the grassland, the earth seemed to stop. A dark blue line shimmered under the pale blue sky. He wondered if that could all be water. Another searching hawk approached in the sky. Artemis stole through the grass back to the woods.

He was relieved to get back to the shelter of the trees. In the shade he found a puddle with fresh water, and he drank breathlessly. He then collected a few acorns from the ground, stuffed them in his cheeks, and climbed up into a hackberry tree. It was an uncomfortable dinner, but at least he was finally able to sit and think. Gradually, darkness descended and he drifted off to sleep.

Artemis was cradled in soft images of cool blue streams, silvery-white birch bark, and crisp mountain air. He saw his mama and his sister, Ellen, smiling. In the background, his papa's rich baritone voice hummed the melody of "Sleep Tight, Sweet Chipmunk."

CHAPTER FOUR
Meeting Reginald

Artemis awoke the next morning in a haze. He blinked his eyes and sniffed the air. His scabby legs ached and itched. There was a moment of confusion, and then realization struck him in the chest. His heart sank.

"Oh, what have I done?" he moaned aloud.

To his surprise a crackly voice answered, "Well, I don't know. What *have* you done?"

Artemis jumped and twirled around on his branch. Below him on the ground, stood a most peculiar looking creature. It was almost the shape of an opossum, but instead of fur it wore a thick, leathery shell and had a long, pointy head.

"Well, what?" the strange armored creature persisted.

"Oh, um. Hello, sir," stuttered Artemis.

The two scrutinized each other for a moment, and then both blurted out at the exact same time, "What *are* you?"

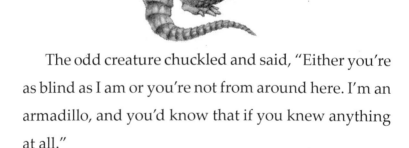

The odd creature chuckled and said, "Either you're as blind as I am or you're not from around here. I'm an armadillo, and you'd know that if you knew anything at all."

"Well, I suppose I'm not from around here. I'm a chipmunk," Artemis replied with as much dignity as he could muster.

"A chipmunk," croaked the armadillo. "Hmmm. Funny little stripes. Like a skunk. Chipmunk. Sounds like skunk, but you don't smell like one."

"Well, I would hope not," Artemis replied.

"No," continued the armadillo, "you have your own distinct scent of sickness, scabs, rancid acorns, and musty canvas." The armored creature took a scornful whiff of the air and nodded in agreement with himself.

Artemis was at a loss for words, so said nothing.

"Yep, armadillos may not see well, but we've got an excellent sense of smell. And so, Chipskunk, what have you done?" The armadillo glanced up and then began scraping the dirt with his claws.

Artemis sighed and said, "Well, my name is Artemis, and well, I do seem to have gotten myself into a predicament. I am quite lost."

Already distracted, the armadillo began circling around at the base of the tree and then continued scratching the dirt.

"What is your name?" asked Artemis.

"Reginald."

After a moment of determined digging, Reginald continued, "Lost, huh? Sounds like you might be in for an adventure then, Chipskunk. And what better place than this? Paradise!" He scratched around some more. "We've got fresh water at Clay Bottom

Pond. There's woods, fields, and even ocean! You've got plenty of seeds, berries, and nuts to eat. There's hardly any people to hide from, and the weather is beautiful."

"Hmm," Artemis muttered doubtfully.

"Lots of acorns from the live oaks. Can't complain."

"Live oaks?"

"Uh, yeah! So, if you're not from around here, then where are you from, Chipskunk?"

"I'm from New Hampshire," replied Artemis.

"Oh yeah? Hamster you say? I met a hamster once. He didn't belong here. Real soft. Didn't last long."

Artemis wasn't sure how to respond.

"Anyway," continued the armadillo, "the obnoxious fox squirrels won't actually hurt you. Just watch out for the hawks and owls, of course. And if you go down to the pond, steer clear of the gators."

"Gators?" Artemis asked.

"Yes, you know, *alligators*," Reginald said condescendingly. "You do know what an alligator is, don't you?"

"Well, I've heard of them in tall tales," Artemis said, "but I've never seen one." He thought of the fantastic stories that his papa recited at gatherings.

The armadillo started to dig even more furiously but managed to mumble, "Keep it that way, Chipskunk."

Reginald was engrossed in his task of digging, and it was clear that the conversation was over. Artemis watched the hole deepen. It was really quite impressive. Wondering whether it was a grub the armadillo was after or just a compulsive habit, Artemis climbed onto a notch on the tree trunk. He watched quietly. He could hear a soft muttering and realized it was the armadillo.

"Digging digging digging digging. Digging digging digging digging," chanted the creature as he scraped the earth.

The hole was magnificent. Artemis continued to watch. The sun was just rising, and slivers of light were beginning to peek through the leaves above. He had managed his first night. Today was a new day. He imagined his mother's voice reminding him, "Anything is possible, Artie dear." Then he thought of his father's frequent response, "But some things are less likely than others."

As his mind wandered, Artemis gazed out around the woods. To his surprise, he noticed a raccoon ambling headfirst down the trunk of a tree. The raccoon was in no hurry. Artemis backed up on his perch and inconspicuously pressed himself against the bark. Timidly, he peered down. Surely Reginald was safe in his shell.

The raccoon was watching the armadillo and almost seemed to smile. Now here was a creature Artemis was at least familiar with. The raccoons that he knew at home were famous for stealing and eating almost anything. The masked bandit quietly approached. He was definitely grinning! With long back legs and short front legs, he hunched way over as he slunk closer. When he was almost behind the furiously digging armadillo, he slowed down and crept even closer. He was practically upon Reginald. Certainly Artemis should say something, but he felt paralyzed.

The armadillo continued his soft muttering, "Digging digging digging digging. Digging digging digging digging."

Suddenly the raccoon crouched down to the ground and let out a deafening shriek. "Chieeeee!"

The unsuspecting armadillo instantly shot straight up into the air, just missing Artemis on his perch.

Artemis screamed and scurried higher into the tree. Peals of laughter rose from the raccoon, who was already loping off. Heart pounding, Artemis peeked down again. Reginald had landed in the same spot he had launched from.

"Good-for-nothing...black-eyed...fur ball... gets me every stinkin' time...one of these days..." The armadillo muttered between breaths. Without looking up or saying more, he shuffled off into the underbrush.

"Well then, um, good-bye," Artemis called timidly. "I'm sorry, I should have, well, I should have warned..." And his shaky voice trailed out. The armadillo was gone.

It was definitely not New Hampshire.

Artemis scanned the area for hawks and other threats. He wondered how many eyes were watching him. He longed for the comfort of his old woods, where he knew every scent. He knew the quiet sound of danger and the warning calls of every bird. Artemis hadn't fully appreciated his summer neighbors, Pell and Carmina. According to his mother, the Baltimore orioles arrived in May each year, first Pell and then Carmina. The males always arrived two days before the females. They would build their nest each spring in one of the tall maple trees near Squam Lake. Once the babies hatched, they guarded that nest night and day. No animal could approach without setting off Carmina and Pell's distinct two-note alarm call. Instantly the babies would be silent, and Artemis, out of habit, would be on guard too. The orioles were as sure as the setting sun. He even missed the crass and chatty gray squirrels who hogged all the acorns, only to bury them and forget. At least their bickering kept him up-to-date. Artemis would somehow have to learn about this new land. He wondered idly about mountain lions, hawks, owls, and snakes. Ellen was always good at spotting a snake from a mile away. He could almost hear her voice, "Snake, Artie, snake!" as she tugged his paw.

Artemis peered out from his perch. He squirmed and chewed at the crusty bites on his legs. The one lone burr still stung his back. If he could just get it out, he might feel a little better. He began to rub his back against the trunk of the tree. Eventually the tenacious stickers caught the bark and slid out from his fur. Carefully, he plucked the burr from the tree and let it fall silently to the ground. It was a sad souvenir from his time with Ellen. Suddenly he was sorry to let it go. Would the seeds inside the burr

 survive and heroically grow here? Or would they go the way of Reginald's hamster friend? And what about Artemis?

The sun rose higher in the sky. Artemis remained in the tree.

He felt rested but incapable of venturing out. Instead he sat, agonizing over the details of his last moments with his sister. He thought about their game, the crackers, and the box. Artemis replayed the memory over and over, wishing he could change the outcome. He imagined Ellen still hiding, waiting for him.

The day passed and turned to night.

CHAPTER FIVE
An Unlikely Find

Morning came. Artemis took a deep breath and finally huffed, "Oh bother. What would Ellen do? No sense in clinging to this tree all day. Adapt, Artie, adapt."

Despite his sore and scabbed legs, he jumped along the sprawling branches and then down onto the ground.

He hopped through the woods, examining the strange prickly bushes and plants. He was careful to avoid the telltale sand piles where he sometimes saw the dreaded ants. One towering hill he passed was over four times his height. The earthy scent of mud and rot was thick, and Artemis knew he was close to a pond.

Surely his family was worried sick by now. "Artie's not one to just abandon his family," his papa would say. Artemis wondered how far and long they would look for him. He tried to put them out of his mind.

As he approached a sunny clearing, something caught his eye. It was a shiny brown form resting on the ground. He peered at it from a distance. It was oddly shaped and seemed out of place. Since there was no one around, he scampered up to it. The rich wood glowed in the sunlight. Four tight strings stretched across a delicately carved bridge. They ran up the long neck to the scroll, where they wrapped around black wooden pegs. Artemis cautiously crept around the instrument.

"A violin. How strange," he thought. There was not a soul in sight. Wondering who could have left such a treasure in such an odd spot, he called out, "Hello! Helloooo? Anybody here?"

No one replied. Artemis tentatively strummed the strings. The violin made a lovely, resonant ripple of sound with a faint buzz. Something rattled inside.

Artemis stretched over the instrument and peeked into one of the beautifully carved holes.

He jumped when a cricket popped out of the other side. "Ooh! Well, now, I'm quite sure you ought not be in there!" Artemis cried.

The cricket disappeared into the leaves before Artemis could ask any questions.

The instrument appeared to be hand-crafted for a small human. Next to the violin lay a matching child-sized bow. There was no case, no music, no stand. Nothing. Not even any trash, the sure signature of humans. The lovely instrument was in remarkably good shape for having been left unprotected. Artemis gently touched the auburn finish. Then, leaving the violin lying in the grass, he picked up the bow. Clutching it with both paws, he set it on the skinniest string and heaved his entire body to one side. The bow scraped across the string, and a piercing, scratchy sound rang out.

"Perhaps a little less force," he thought. He drew the bow again, more gently this time. A prettier tone emerged. Artemis experimented, playing each of the four strings. Then he set the bow down, and on tiptoes he leaned his body across the shiny wood face of the violin. He was careful not to scratch the finish. Stretched out across it, he could pluck and strum the strings. With each sound he felt the vibrations tickle his belly. He then picked up the bow and tried it again. There just wasn't a way for him to play any notes other than the open strings. He was simply too small. Still, he was fascinated.

After several hours of tinkering, he knew he should move on. He just could not bear to leave the instrument.

Artemis picked up the scroll and started dragging the violin. Although light, it was many times his size. Clutching both the bow and violin at the same time was difficult. With each bump and scrape, the instrument let out a resonant thump and ring. He quickly realized this was a bad idea. It was far too delicate an instrument to be dragged along the ground. What Artemis needed was a way to transport the violin.

CHAPTER SIX

In Search

Artemis scurried around the woods looking for ideas. Soon the trees abruptly cleared, and he found himself by the steep bank of a pond. In the middle of the pond stood a very small island. Artemis was immediately struck by the sight before him. Crowding the island trees were hundreds of birds. There were tall, elegant white ones, huge, blue-gray giants, and black birds with snakelike necks. The strangest, though, were the bright pink birds. These were not the sleek and dainty birds of the mountains. They were enormous creatures with long pink legs, pink feathers, a white neck, and a large, squashed-looking beak. A few of the pink birds were standing in the pond, swishing their giant flat bills back and forth in the water. The island hummed with a cacophony of grunting sounds. Artemis struggled to get his bearings and quickly decided that the odd noise was coming from the birds. He hopped closer to the water.

A great, honking voice suddenly called out, "Never seen a spoonbill before, hon?"

Startled, Artemis looked up to see one of the giant pink birds perched in a tree next to him.

"Oh! No. I most definitely have not seen anyone like you before," he replied in awe.

"Well that goes for both of us, hon. What kind of rodent are you?"

"I'm a chipmunk," he called up to her.

"Hmm, a chipmunk…Don't think I've ever seen anyone like you around here. At least not with those stripes. Quite distinctive, I suppose."

Artemis puffed up a little bit. Then he deflated at the thought of being alone.

As if reading his mind, she asked, "Just you, hon? Where are you from?"

"Um, New Hampshire. I'm from New Hampshire,

and my name is Artemis. Where am I, if you don't mind my asking?"

"Oh, hon," the great bird answered, "you're in Texas. This is High Island. The Gulf of Mexico is just over there." She nodded her flat beak to the south. "I've never been up north, but I know this area well. Been here for all nine years of my life."

"My goodness," marveled Artemis. "So, you don't migrate anywhere?"

"Well, hon, that's a good question. I don't. Some spoonbills do. My husband and I live here." She pointed to a similar-looking enormous pink bird in a tree.

"Well, um, I don't imagine you know anyone from New Hampshire, do you?" Artemis asked hopefully.

"I sure don't, hon." The bird picked at the pink fluff under her giant wing, twitched, and shook out her feathers again.

Artemis felt the pull of the instrument he had left behind. He had one more question. "Mrs. Spoonbill, would you by any chance be missing a violin?"

She stopped smoothing her feathers and regarded him, "Florence, hon. You can call me Flo. But oh goodness me, a violin? No. I haven't the dexterity in these wings to play the violin."

Artemis nodded sheepishly, but she continued, "Always did want to play the trumpet, though."

He eyed her long bill doubtfully.

"Well, Artemis-hon, I'm a busy bird and really must get going. But you take care. Watch out for the alligators and all. There's one big one. This is his territory. He doesn't like anyone in Clay Bottom Pond. That's good for us," she nodded to the island where giant nests clogged the trees, "but bad for you. You don't want to hang around this pond, hon."

The bird flapped away, and Artemis gazed into the water. All he saw was his reflection. The black and tan stripes along his back looked bright against his acorn-brown fur. His ears were soft and delicate with a slight touch of pink inside. His sides pulsed quickly with each breath he took. He had seen himself before. What startled him was the sudden impression of smallness. He looked utterly tiny. It was both unexpected and disconcerting.

Artemis wandered back into the woods and away from the pond. He wondered if his family had slept last night. He wondered how many of his friends were searching for him. The car ride with the humans had lasted several days and the distance was unfathomable. He wished that he could just let his family know he was alive.

The violin was a welcome distraction from his concerns. On his walk he collected a large piece of bark and piled it with sticks and soft moss. Slowly he dragged the supplies back to his spot. The instrument was as he had left it, lying temptingly in the weeds. Once again he scurried around the violin, checking it over. He would need to build some kind of sled for it.

Artemis examined the sticks and bark and then set off to look for some twine. The bushes nearby were covered with a tangle of vines. He clawed free as many strands as he could.

By late afternoon Artemis was exhausted but glad to have a mission. Using the vines, bark, and sticks, he wove a violin-sized sled. Then he added a cushy layer of furry moss to the surface. It was a perfect bed for the violin and bow. At the front, he tied a strong loop of vines that he could wear as a harness. He tried out the empty sled. It did not move smoothly. Something was missing. Artemis ran into the tall grass and chewed off two of the widest stalks he could find. The grass was sharp and tough. It felt smooth when he stroked it upward, but jagged going downward. They would be perfect to use as runners if he attached them in the right direction. He hoisted the sled up and rolled it over. Being careful not to slice himself with the grass, he stretched the blades out along the underside of the sled and tucked them in at each end. Once the blades were secure, he rolled the sled back over so that it was upright on its new runners. Artemis tried out his invention before putting in the violin. It slid miraculously! It would, however, only go backward.

With a frustrated sigh, he hoisted the sled over, ripped out the blades of grass and set them beside the sled. He then reattached them in what he hoped was the opposite direction. Artemis tried out the invention a second time.

"Argh!" he shouted. One blade was attached right and one was going in the wrong direction. It was like having permanent brakes on.

"Persistence is the key to success," he imagined his papa telling him. Artemis ground his teeth and

started again.

On the third try, he reattached the blades and told himself, "Third time's a charm!"

The third time was, apparently, not a charm. It was irritating and exhausting. Almost as exasperating as when on the fourth try, Artemis found that the blades were facing perfectly backward again.

"Argh!" He sat down and stewed. After collecting his thoughts, he continued. Rather than taking the blades off, he untied the harness straps from the front and reattached them to the back of the sled. The back became the front!

Finally, it was perfect. Artemis strapped in the violin and tried dragging the sled. Although cumbersome and heavy, it slid nicely over the ground.

Lugging his treasure behind him, Artemis trudged across the field in search of a safe place to sleep.

CHAPTER SEVEN

The Voice of an Angel

The violin lay safely on its bed while Artemis panted in his harness. The air was thick with mosquitos, and the clouds were a heavy gray. He followed a dirt path for lack of any other ideas. When the sled became unbearably heavy, he stopped and climbed out of his tethers.

Suddenly there was a horrendous screeching, "Kidee-kidee! Kidee-kidee!"

Out of the brush ran a screaming bird. She was brown with a white belly, and she had two black stripes around her neck as though she wore two

45

collars. He had seen killdeer like her once or twice up north but never spoken with one.

"Kidee-kidee!" She shrieked again. Then, flapping, she ran by him and started dragging her right wing. She lurched around, her injured wing hanging awkwardly.

"My goodness! Are you all right?" Artemis asked.

She staggered farther away, so he followed her, leaving the violin.

"Kidee-kidee!" she screamed.

"Well now, really, I can't help you if you keep running away."

She cocked her head to the side and peered at him suspiciously with one eye. "Help me? Help me? You can help me by getting away from here!"

"Um, okay, but do you need anything? I mean, your wing—it's, well…" As Artemis spoke, it seemed that she was tucking her wing back up into place. It looked immediately restored. "Oh, I just thought you needed help," he said.

"And I thought you were going to trample my eggs, my eggs, with that thing you're dragging!" she screeched.

He was taken aback. "Well, what good does running around with a broken wing do?"

"I don't know. Just never mind, never mind. You scared me is all," she told him, calming down.

Artemis turned and headed back to the violin.

The killdeer twittered along behind him, calling out, "Just watch it, watch it!"

Artemis nodded and tried to reassure her. "But where are the eggs?" he asked.

"Right there! Right there! Watch it! Watch it!" Once again, she was in a frenzy.

Artemis searched the ground in front of him, but all he saw were three small rocks by the sled. At least they looked like rocks. He examined them carefully and realized they were, in fact, speckled, gray eggs.

They looked just like the gravel in the path.

"Oh!" he gasped. "I see, my goodness. Um, Mrs. Killdeer, no offense, but do you really think that was a good place to lay your eggs? Right here on the side of the path, in full view?"

She was settling down again but still a bit huffy. "Well, *you* didn't see them!"

"Hmm, I guess I didn't," Artemis agreed.

"What are you doing here anyway? You look like a lost reindeer with his sleigh," she told him.

Artemis looked at her blankly.

"Oh, never mind, never mind," she squawked. "What are you? A squirrel?"

Artemis took a deep breath. "Close enough. A type of squirrel," he sighed. "Mrs. Killdeer, you wouldn't know whose violin this is, would you?"

"Nobody I know," she answered. "Certainly not mine. I mean, let's be practical here. I'm strong, but I'm no giant, no giant." The killdeer shook her head spastically. "By the way, my name is BB. Just BB."

Artemis nodded, and she went on, "Anyway, who needs a violin? I'm a singer. I've been told I have the voice of an angel!" With that she ran off screaming, "Kidee-kidee!"

To Artemis's surprise, he saw her sprinting down the path toward a familiar-looking masked face.

BB shrieked at the approaching raccoon and danced around him in a frenzy. Then she turned and dragged her wing and started limping in the opposite direction from Artemis and the eggs. The curious raccoon loped after her. Artemis watched as they worked their way farther and farther away. Then like magic she rose up and flew. She was gone.

The raccoon skulked off.

A few moments later, the bird quietly reappeared across the path from Artemis and her eggs.

"I think I know him," said Artemis. "He's a bit of a prankster, isn't he?"

The killdeer looked aghast. "He's a murderer! A

murderer!" she spat. Keeping her voice as low as she could, she told Artemis about the four eggs that the beast had stolen and eaten last year. "My eggs, the beast, the beast!" She shook her head angrily. "Well, let him head down there to the marshland. There's a tern colony," she muttered.

"Oh," said Artemis uncomfortably. "Can he get at their eggs?" he worried. "Maybe we should do something."

"No, no!" she squawked. "They might not even have eggs yet. It's still early for them. Don't go over there. It won't be pretty. It won't be pretty."

Despite her warnings, Artemis scampered away and hopped up onto a tree stump. This way he could peer at the raccoon, who was ambling toward the marshy grassland. Raccoons, he knew, were no fools. They were, in fact, extremely intelligent, but he suspected that this one was young.

Artemis felt his heart stop when he saw the raccoon make a small careful circle, inspecting the ground. The bandit then stopped and picked something up. Even from a distance, Artemis could see it was an egg. Before he could move, screaming birds filled the air.

"Oyt oyt oyt! Oyt oyt oyt!" they shrieked, instantly

rising up in one great, churning cloud. The swarm dipped down, and a few stragglers dive-bombed the raccoon. The mass rose again, folded in on itself, twisted apart, and gracefully looped around again.

"Oyt oyt oyt!" The terns swirled the sky in an angry blur, and suddenly there was white poop raining down, splatting like wet paint. The raccoon ran, no longer carrying the egg.

Artemis scurried back to the killdeer and the violin.

"Wow, you weren't kidding!"

"Kidding? Kidding? Do I look like a kidding bird? Listen, I know you mean well, but you'd better take that instrument of yours and move on before my husband comes back to watch the nest, the nest."

There really was no nest, but Artemis nodded.

"Otherwise," she went on, "we'll be doing the whole rigmarole again."

They bid their good-byes, and Artemis carefully dragged his treasure around the three little eggs.

CHAPTER EIGHT
A Hard Rain

As he made his way along the path, Artemis could smell the distinct scent of campfire and cooking meat. Wary of humans, he dragged the violin into the bushes and scampered up an oak tree to get a better view. In a clearing to the north, he saw a small fire and the two humans he had ridden with. In the woods to the west of them stood a brown tent. He was at a safe distance and decided to settle on a high branch of the tree. He ate the strange acorns and licked his scabby legs. It was becoming dark, and the humidity was oppressive. It was going to rain.

Artemis gasped. "Rain! The violin! Oh no!"

He had to protect it. His mind raced, and he searched for a way to cover the instrument. Seeing nothing, he scurried down the tree. He darted from bush to bush looking for ideas. In a panic he strapped on the vines and began to pull the sled. He dragged it deeper into the woods until he reached the brown tent. Cautiously he scanned the area. The humans were out of sight but probably still at the campfire.

A warm, fat raindrop landed on Artemis's nose. Another splatted onto the face of the violin. There was no time. The drops quickened around him. Artemis poked his head into the tent, and seeing no one, he pulled the violin in. The smell was sickeningly familiar. Inside were two outstretched sleeping bags and some clothes hanging out of a backpack. He looked around, bitterly ignoring the cursed jar of crackers.

He grabbed a soft sock and tenderly dried off the violin. He knew he should not be in the tent, but he needed something waterproof. He could leave the violin in the tent for the humans, but somehow Artemis couldn't stand the thought. It hadn't been in the car with them. Surely it wasn't theirs.

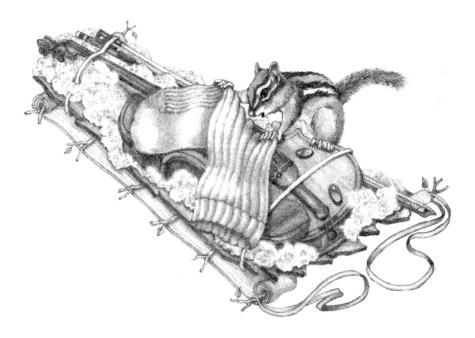

The floor of the tent was a smooth polyester fabric. If he could just pull it up and take part of it with him, he could wrap it around the violin. The humans would be back soon. He frantically scurried around the tent, trying to release any part of the fabric. He ran back outside and found that there were stakes holding each corner down. He dug and pulled at one and managed to work it free. He raced to the next stake and yanked. The floor tarp was barely coming loose. He ran to another stake and desperately tugged. Even after freeing the third stake, the fabric of the tent was still intact. He couldn't possibly chew it apart in time. He tugged and gnawed open a back window flap, but even that wouldn't rip off. Overwhelmed, Artemis rummaged through the backpack of clothes, yanking out shirts and pants in a frenzy. Finally, he discovered a wad of dirty laundry encased in a clear plastic bag. That was it! He heaved out the stinky clothes and admired the beautiful bag.

Listening carefully, Artemis scurried over to the sled, untied the violin and bow, and worked them both into the bag. The fit was perfect. He tied the plastic in a tight knot and then strapped it all back into the sled. The rain began to pour down harder outside. The humans would be on their way back. Artemis harnessed up and quickly hauled the sled out into the woods. He immediately pulled the instrument behind the tent so that he would be out of the path of the returning humans. There was no more smell of smoke, only warm, earthy rain. Despite the downpour, the violin lay dry in its clear, plastic bubble on the sled.

Suddenly there was a rustling as something entered the tent from the front. Artemis froze.

CHAPTER NINE
The Chase

Through the gaping back window of the tent, two black, masked eyes locked onto his own.

"Well, well, what have we here?" a silky voice rang out over the rain. The raccoon was staring him down while deftly unscrewing the jar of crackers. Artemis knew he wasn't referring to the food in the jar; in fact, he opened it with the casual ease of ownership. "You think," the raccoon went on, "that I haven't seen you spying on me and poking around in my woods. Well, I've got news for you. It was a mistake to let you go last time. I may make mistakes, but I never make the same one twice."

Artemis stood, unable to think of what to say.

"And that ridiculous instrument you're dragging around! You know that if anyone here could really play that silly thing, it would be me."

Artemis's horror was doubled as he saw two feeble lights approaching in the rain.

"I'll get you!" growled the raccoon. Still holding the jar, the beast lunged toward the window.

Over the course of the next second, many things happened. Artemis twirled around and sprang. The harness dug into him, and he remembered he was still attached. It pulled him down, and he scrambled to try to get out of it. The twine tightened across his chest and tangled painfully around his ankle. He struggled forward, unable to free himself. The sled followed behind him, however. Closing the cracker jar, the raccoon jumped again at the window and started to climb out. There was a ripping and swishing sound, and the chipmunk turned to see the tent sway ponderously and collapse onto the raccoon. Artemis pulled with all his strength and ran. The sled bumped along behind him, and the vine cut deeper into his ankle. When he glanced behind him, he saw the soaked tent shifting in a writhing, muddy heap. The raccoon thrashed underneath it, trying to release himself. The still-approaching flashlight dots began to bounce. Artemis ran. He was faster than a raccoon, he knew, but not when tied to an enormous instrument.

He blundered blindly through the woods. Behind him flew the sled, with the violin still in place. He raced over wet grass and leaves and through muddy puddles.

The raccoon had freed himself and was hulking after him, still holding the cracker jar under one arm. No humans could be seen. Artemis wheezed with the pressure of the vines on his chest, but he didn't dare slow down. He ran and ran.

The gap between them was closing. Artemis tore through the woods and out into a clearing.

"You're mine now, chipmunk!" Artemis heard

from directly behind him.

Suddenly he was sliding and tumbling down a slope, and with a splash he landed in water. Tangled and drowning, Artemis struggled to get his head to the surface. Waves from a second impact sent him into a spin under the water. He couldn't tell which way was up. He saw nothing but blackness as his body was tossed and pummeled against the sled. He clawed at the strangling vines.

Then, miraculously, Artemis's head was above water, and he gasped for air and choked. The pounding rain drowned out the sound of his coughing. He managed to turn and pry his leg out from one of the tethers. He kicked his paws and frantically swam. He was free!

The violin had fallen out of its sled and was floating in the bubble of plastic. The sled was now a raft, bobbing separately on the surface of the water. Next to it was the raccoon. Only his head and cracker jar poked out of the black water as he circled the raft, searching for his prey. Artemis paddled around the violin and hid while trying to catch his breath. They had somehow ended up quite far from the shore. Artemis was glad to be able to swim, but he was no match for a raccoon. He peered across the pond in desperation.

The raccoon was between Artemis and the nearest shore. Rain continued to pelt down on the water, filling the dark with a constant roar. The bandit circled the raft once more and then began swimming toward the violin and Artemis.

"I know you're there, and trust me, I can see in the dark quite well," growled the voice, with no hint of exertion.

Artemis had nowhere to go. He tried to swim away from shore while keeping the violin between them, but the raccoon was coming too quickly. Artemis had only a matter of seconds. He paddled his legs wildly, to no avail. He was too slow.

"Give it up, chipmunk!" called the raccoon. "I could swim all night. Can you? I know you're behind there. Oh, there you are!"

Artemis looked back in terror.

Just then a dark form swept up behind the bandit. Massive jaws snapped around the raccoon, and there was an instant of thrashing. The enormous shape in the water began to spin like a whirlwind, creating violent waves and spray. Artemis squinted into the darkness, desperately trying to see what was happening. The water rushed around him, and he struggled to keep from getting sucked down into the swirling currents. The frenzy did not last long. With a few quick jerks, both raccoon and predator were gone.

The violin bubble bobbed and glistened in the dark. The glass jar of crackers danced on the surface of the water closer to shore.

Suddenly aware of his naked paws and belly dangling in the water, Artemis swam to the violin. He clung to the tied end and clambered up the slippery plastic covering the scroll. He teetered up the neck and positioned himself on the bridge. He hung on, willing the puffed-out plastic to hold.

The waves cleared, and the rain diminished abruptly. It was suddenly quiet. Artemis wondered if it was the calm before the storm. He didn't dare climb off the violin. The dark water rippled only slightly around him.

He waited.

Then out of the water in front of him rose two glowing golden eyes and an enormous pair of cave-like nostrils. Artemis crouched, frozen and wide-eyed. Only the pulse in his throat twitched rhythmically. He

felt the water move ever so slightly under his float. The enormous eyes stared at his. Silently the head rose out of the black, and Artemis could see mountains of ridges along the alligator's long nose. Behind the head a long, extending line of bumps in the water's surface appeared, giving only the subtlest suggestion of astounding size.

Artemis balanced weakly on the floating instrument. The giant jaws opened. Artemis's feeble muscles clenched.

Time—everything—seemed to stop. Artemis felt somehow suspended in the sickening moment. The image of powerful, grimy teeth was burned into his mind. In the distance an ethereal whistle rang out in the dark. It was the angelic call of a single bird. The world around Artemis was calm, and his horror softened. The bird's soothing voice was the reassuring call of an afterlife, or perhaps a past life, or just a calming mechanism of his mind. The past and future blurred together in a strangely peaceful wash as time stood still.

Suddenly the time snag broke, and the jaws stretched into a grin. The reptile's voice bellowed, "Well, bless your heart, you found my violin!"

Artemis was unable to respond or even move.

"How in the world did you bring it out here? Oh, we'd better get it up onto land before that bag up and pops!" the alligator boomed.

Ever so gently, the giant took the knotted end of the bag in his teeth.

They glided through the water, Artemis still perched on the bridge. When the alligator guided them up onto the muddy ground, Artemis sprang off. Relief rushed over his body in the form of uncontrollable shaking. He panted and coughed, while trying to brush the water off his face.

The alligator slowly crawled up the bank, revealing the full length of his massive body and tail. "Little rodent, do you have a name? Can you speak?"

Artemis answered in a tiny trembling voice, "Yes, I…ah…um…My name is Artemis."

The alligator rumbled, "Very nice name. I'm Magnus. It's a pleasure to meet you. And I thank you for bringing me my violin."

"Oh, well, um…it's…it's nice to meet you too, Magnus," Artemis stammered. He wrapped his paws around his chest to repress a shudder. Then he took a deep breath.

CHAPTER TEN

A Place to Rest

The night was quiet and still. Artemis slowly regained his composure. The two sat together on the muddy bank, and Artemis told Magnus of his long adventure.

"You look like you need some rest," Magnus told him. "Why don't you sleep now? Nobody's going to bother you here. Trust me."

Artemis climbed farther up the bank and nestled into some leaves. He watched the motionless alligator, beached on the mud. He thought about his family and wondered if they would ever believe him if he ever got the chance to tell them.

Then he was asleep.

Morning came in what seemed like an instant. The sun was bright on the water, and the spoonbills were croaking and rasping away. Artemis leapt up. He was surprised to see the alligator still asleep in the same spot.

"Magnus, I'm hungry. I'm going to find some food," Artemis said gently, unsure if he should wake the alligator.

"Yeah, yeah," mumbled the giant, not moving a muscle. The massive body lay outstretched, melting into the dirt. His right front claw rested on the tied-off end of the plastic bag, which still held the violin.

Artemis bounced into the woods, where he found dozens of wonderfully tangy and exotic-tasting seeds. He climbed to the tops of trees and marveled at the gnarly shape of the branches. He gazed out at the woods and the pond. The spoonbills and egrets were bustling on the banks of the water and honking in the freshly leafed trees. Steam radiated off the damp ground. Up in New Hampshire ice was just thawing, but here spring was raging. He breathed in the dense warm air and wished that his sister could taste it too. "Oh, Ellen," he sighed.

He knew that he should dig out a burrow to live in and start collecting nuts for a cache, but he was too distracted with his surroundings. More than that, building a burrow meant that he was not going home, and he couldn't think about that. Tomorrow he would figure out a plan. Tomorrow would be the day. He pictured Ellen waiting for him. He couldn't bear the thought of his family combing the woods looking for him. Tomorrow he would do something. He shook his head, thinking about the utter hopelessness of ever getting home.

The only thing Artemis could motivate himself to do was return to Magnus and his violin. After finding some mysterious, but delicious, oblong nuts, he stuffed a couple in his cheeks and darted back to the pond.

As he approached, Artemis became nervous. He had been gone half the morning, but the alligator lay sprawled out in the exact position as the night before, one claw still resting on the bag.

"Magmif," he said and then spit out the large nuts from his cheeks. "Are you okay?" He scurried around the alligator with concern.

Magnus opened one eye and looked at him. "Well, of course I am. What did you think? I was dead?"

"Oh. Well then, okay. Good," Artemis tittered with relief. "When will you get up? When will you play for me?" he asked eagerly.

The alligator opened his other eye and grumbled "I *am* up."

CHAPTER ELEVEN
Music

Gently carrying the violin in his mouth, Magnus crawled up the bank. Artemis scampered ahead, darting up and back, unsure where they were going. Once they reached a grassy area, Magnus stopped and set the violin down.

"I don't like to play where anybody will hear me, and I definitely don't want any other alligators listening. That would just be inviting them, and this is *my* territory," he said ominously. "Now what would you like to hear?"

Magnus ripped open the plastic bag and removed

the instrument. He set it on the ground and began strumming the open strings. Bracing the violin with his left arm, he used his right claw to grip each tuning peg and gently twist, adjusting the pitch. When he was satisfied, he grinned and said, "Usually I just like to improvise. You know what that means? It's when you make it up as you go along. But I know some common songs. My favorite is 'Froggy Went a Courtin'.' You know it?"

With great effort, Magnus reared upright and sat back on his tail and hind legs. He raised the violin and, bending his enormous head down, nestled the instrument under his jaw. His front right claws clutched the bow, and his front left claws wrapped around the neck of the violin. He began to play.

It was a thrilling sound. Artemis was tickled to hear the piercing melody ringing out. He laughed and laughed. With every note the tension of the last few days eased. Excitedly, he joined in singing,

Froggy went a-courtin' and he did ride a-huh, a-huh,
Froggy went a-courtin' and he did ride a-huh, a-huh,
Froggy went a-courtin' and he did ride,
Sword and pistol by his side a-huh, a-huh, a-huh.

Seeing it was a hit, Magnus soared through verse after verse. Artemis crooned on about marrying Miss Mousie and getting Uncle Rat's consent. By the fifteenth verse, "Little black tick, ate so much it made him sick," Artemis was dancing and frolicking too much to sing. Magnus's melody line was jerking with his own heaves of laughter.

When he could play no more, the alligator put the violin down and tried to catch his breath.

"Oh, Magnus, do another, do another!" Artemis tittered.

They sang and played "Little Robin Redbreast," then "Mister Rabbit," and finally, "The Bear Went over the Mountain."

They were tired but content in the warm grass.

"You play wonderfully," Artemis said. "Maybe you should play for all the other animals in the woods."

"Oh, it's not like that," replied Magnus. "I've got nothing to prove. No grand illusions of enlightening the beasts. My music is for me. Anyway, I don't play well and never will, but I still like it. Mama was right. It takes consistent practice to get good."

"Well, you could practice, right?"

The alligator shrugged lazily and said, "Nah, I'm just not like that. It's an alligator thing. I'm not one to go hunt around for work to do. I let it come to me. You know, just like that raccoon. Then I'm quick. Snap! And then I rest. It's not conducive to learning to play an instrument."

"I see." Artemis nodded. "What about that raccoon, anyway? Did you have to eat him?"

Magnus looked surprised and replied, "Well, no. I didn't *have* to, but I did. That's just the way it is. He shouldn't have been in the pond, and I do eat. You know, I protect the nesting birds on that island. Except when I eat them. But usually I don't."

Artemis looked at him nervously.

"Look," Magnus continued, "you don't get to

be a thousand pounds by nibbling on algae and mosquitoes."

"You're not hungry now, are you Magnus?" Artemis asked uneasily.

"Oh, come on, give me some credit. I have great restraint. The truth is, I don't even eat that much. About once a week. That's the good thing about being cold-blooded."

"Hmm," said Artemis.

"Anyway," Magnus reassured him, "if it's any consolation, I don't think chipmunk is on Mama's list of approved eatin'. I think it would'a been between Chihuahua and chipped beef."

Artemis didn't ask if squirrel was on the list.

Magnus closed his eyes and sighed. "You ever had chipped beef, Artemis? You'll have to try it."

Artemis stretched his legs until they twitched and quivered, and then relaxed. "Seems unlikely, Magnus," he said with a yawn.

CHAPTER TWELVE
Magnus

"I reckon it's nap time," announced Magnus. "Let's head back to Clay Bottom. Come on."

The two ambled through the grass, Magnus once again carrying the violin. As they walked, Artemis studied the alligator's gnarled claws.

"Magnus, do you only have four toes on your back legs?"

"Well, yeah," Magnus answered. "Gators are born with four toes in back and five in front. I kinda lost one on the right side, though." He shoved a scarred back leg out for Artemis to see. Sure enough, the fourth toe was just a mangled nub. "Hurricane accident. I'm lucky to have five in the front. Good for violin."

After lumbering partway down the bank, the alligator stopped and pulled away some dead branches. Behind them was a small cave dug into the dirt. In the dry interior lay an open violin case. Magnus carefully laid the violin in the case and closed the lid.

It was midafternoon, and hot.

"Definitely nap time," the alligator mumbled. He crawled down to the waterline and relaxed into the mud. "Ah, that's good." His tail stretched into the water while his head rested on the dirt.

Artemis sat just beyond the water's reach. He felt antsy and wondered if he could actually sleep. He watched as the alligator's eyes closed.

Out of the blue, Artemis blurted out, "We were playing hide-and-seek, Ellen and I. She was hiding, and I never came back."

"What are you talking about?" Magnus asked, eyes opening.

"Well, you know, before I left, or got packed up and taken. We were playing. The worst part of it is that she probably thought I was ditching her. I wonder how long she hid, waiting," Artemis whimpered.

"Maybe she still is," Magnus suggested.

"Is that supposed to make me feel better, Magnus?"

"Well, I don't know. Do you want me to make you feel better? I'm an alligator. I don't usually make animals feel better."

Artemis had to laugh.

"Look," said Magnus, "I'm sure she figured out something happened. Has that been eating away at you this whole time?"

"Well, yeah," Artemis admitted. He sighed in frustration.

"You'll figure something out," Magnus reassured him.

"I can't imagine what, but we'll see. For now, I think I'll go find some food. You sleep."

When Artemis returned, the sun was a blazing orange orb at the bottom of the sky. All the clouds in the west glowed bright pink and gold, and the pond reflected the colors in a distorted shimmer. Magnus lay in his same spot, but his eyes were open.

"You certainly are a busy little rodent. Did you find anything good?"

"Oh yes. Absolutely. Look at these nuts. I found even more of them." Artemis showed Magnus the smooth oblong nuts that he had discovered.

"Those are pecans. You never had them before? You should taste pecan pie."

"Pie?"

"A human child once dropped a chunk of it, and I got to taste it once they left," explained Magnus.

"Wow. No, I haven't even heard of pecans. They're *so* good! I wish Ellen—well, they're really good." Artemis paused and then continued, "I just don't know. It's all so different here. I mean, it's amazing, but I don't know. I guess I don't know what to do."

"Why do you have to do anything?" Magnus asked.

"Well, I don't know. It's just not home."

Artemis sat down on a rock by the alligator's huge head, and suddenly his eyes blurred with tears.

"Oh, hey. I hear ya," said the alligator. "But you know, when things get weird, little buddy, you improvise. Sometimes it's the only thing *to* do. A few years ago, we had a terrible drought. I hunkered down in a deep burrow that I made. The water in this pond gradually dried up, until there was nothing but dry, cracked clay. The fish died, the birds moved, and there was nothing but me and a bunch of black vultures. Artemis, do you know why a vulture has a bald head? So he can stick it inside a carcass and—"

"*Magnus*! Oh, come on! What did you do?"

"Well," the alligator continued, "I walked. I walked a long way. Eventually I found a slough with a bit of mud, and that led me to a pond that had a little more water. Many animals died. Toward the end of the drought, the humans did something amazing. It was strange. I heard it from the egrets. They said the humans were pumping in millions of gallons of water to Clay Bottom Pond. I didn't totally believe it, but I came back. Sure enough, fresh water! It was just in time. The migrating birds were on their way, crossing over the Gulf of Mexico, and they needed a place to stop. It took a long time for the fish to repopulate, but they did." Magnus shook his head, remembering. "I didn't eat for almost a year, you know."

"No!" gasped Artemis.

"Yes," Magnus said solemnly.

"Wow! I didn't know anybody could live that long without food."

"Well, you survive, or you don't. Even stranger was the hurricane that hit several years ago." Magnus was on a roll now. "The ocean came up onto the land and flooded this whole area. There was salt water mixed with rain water covering the land. Everyone was lost for a long time."

"Really? A hurricane?"

"Oh yes! It was hideous. I swam for two days, just trying to survive and find a place to go."

"You can really swim in ocean water, Magnus?"

"Well, sure I can, but it's not good. During that time this whole area became a highway for swimmers. Everyone was lost, and many died. Horrible. That's when I found my violin, though."

"And lost your toe?"

"Yep. But that's another story."

Artemis looked around him at the peaceful pond and flourishing animal life. He had never seen hurricanes or droughts of that severity, nor could he even imagine it. He pictured his burrow in New Hampshire.

"Magnus, do you think I'll ever get home?"

The great alligator looked serious. "That's what I'm saying, little buddy. Maybe you will; maybe you won't. There probably are other chipmunks in Texas. You could look for them, you could stay here, or you could find a way back to New Hampshire. You're just gonna have to improvise."

They sat on the bank of the pond and watched a bright orange and black butterfly flit around a log.

Staring at it, Artemis mused, "You know, my papa told me about monarchs. If it survives, that butterfly will have babies who might make it up to my home state. They won't even know their own parents. Every fourth generation or so migrates north. Did you know that, Magnus?"

Magnus shook his head.

Artemis continued, "I wonder what they do during droughts and hurricanes. Maybe they improvise."

The two observed the butterfly thoughtfully.

"Magnus, were you born from an egg?"

"Oh sure, I was," the alligator rumbled.

Artemis nodded, but it was hard to imagine the fifteen-foot-long creature as a tiny hatching baby.

"Yep, there were forty-seven of us boys, not counting the red-bellied sliders, of course."

"Wait, the *who*?" asked Artemis.

"The turtles. It was funny, because just after we hatched there were all these tiny turtles that hatched too. Some mother turtle had sneaked in and laid her eggs in with Mama's. Well, the eggs survived, but a lot of the baby turtles got eaten once they hatched. I may only be remembering the story and not the actual event. It was forty-nine years ago, but I do still picture it."

"Holy roly-poly, Magnus! You're forty-nine? Hah...I'm one." Artemis squeaked.

Magnus chuckled. "Yep, my brothers and I stayed with Mama for more than a year. Some of them were eaten by other alligators, but we did pretty well. Mama was good to us."

"No sisters?"

"Nope," said Magnus. "The nest was hot, so we were all boys."

CHAPTER THIRTEEN
A *Familiar* Voice

The two friends sat together, just thinking. The continuous drone of the spoonbills and egrets blurred into a peaceful ostinato in the background.

Suddenly Artemis was aware of one single melodic thread drifting through the texture. The voice was lovely and clear as it whistled a slurred call. It was so familiar, so peaceful. Just as before, when Magnus and Artemis had first met in the pond, time seemed to stop. Artemis pictured Magnus's teeth, the dark shimmering water, Ellen, and his burrow in New Hampshire. The voice stopped and then rose again from the far side of the pond.

Barely breathing, Artemis listened in a trance. An image of a giant maple tree drifted into his mind. And Pell!

Artemis gasped and woke with a start.

"Pell. Pell!" he cried. "Oh my stars, it's Pell!"

Magnus jerked his head up in confusion. "Whah? Huh?"

"Oh, Magnus, Magnus, it's Pell! It's got to be. But how?"

"What are you talking about?" the alligator asked.

"I know that bird. He's a Baltimore oriole. We have to find him! Come on! It sounds like he's all the way on the other side. I have to run around the pond!"

Artemis frantically listened for the call again.

"No," said Magnus, quickly understanding. "I have a quicker way. Hop on." The alligator got to his feet. With his long nose, he scooped up the chipmunk and flipped him up onto his great head. With surprising speed, he darted into the pond.

They glided through the water with ease. Artemis crouched just behind Magnus's enormous nostrils. The ride was smooth and fast as the alligator's powerful tail swished side to side.

"Hurry Magnus! I can't hear him!"

Magnus raised his head a bit and growled, "Little buddy, I should probably tell you that if I sneeze you're going to go flying, so quit tickling my nose."

"I'm just trying to hang on," pleaded Artemis.

"Well, you're making me cross-eyed. Can you get behind my eyes?"

Artemis crept up the speeding reptile's snout and carefully climbed between his eyes and onto the top of his head. There he perched, clinging to the ridges behind the alligator's protruding eyes.

Magnus lifted his head again long enough to mutter, "Much better. Now where is this Pell?"

"I don't know. I think I heard him just ahead. Oh, I have to find him!"

They cut through the water at breathtaking speed.

A tiny flash of orange flew out from the trees but then disappeared back into the woods.

As the pair approached the bank of the pond, Artemis began yelling, "Pell! Pell! Please, Pell!"

There was no sign of him.

"Please, Pell! Come back, Pell!" Artemis cried, but his voice was small, and the pond and woods were large.

"Oh no, no, no! Pell! Come back!" Artemis shrieked.

Magnus crawled up the bank and out of the water. Artemis hunched in despair on his head.

Suddenly a familiar voice honked, "Well, I'll be! Life is full of surprises. What in the world are you doing, hon?"

It was not the bird they were looking for, but the same spoonbill Artemis had met earlier. She sat perched in a tree above them.

"Oh, Flo," Artemis whimpered, "I heard a friend. He's an oriole. He was here, and now he's gone. Oh, I need to catch up with him."

She shook her enormous bill and looked at the pair doubtfully.

"I think it's someone I know," Artemis whined.

"Well hon, maybe I can help. What's his name?"

"Pell. He's Pell," Artemis said, hopefully.

The spoonbill fluttered off her branch and flapped out over the water. With legs and neck jutting straight out, she flew heavily, as if with great effort. She circled back and up over the trees, honking loudly.

Other excited spoonbills began honking as well, and there was no hope of Artemis hearing the lovely voice he longed for.

Magnus and Artemis soon lost track of where she had gone.

They waited. Artemis hopped down onto the ground and scanned the trees. There was no sign of either bird.

"This is crazy," Artemis moaned. "Maybe I'm just going crazy. Magnus, I'm sorry."

"Well, I don't know, little buddy, we'll see. It's okay."

"What am I thinking?"

"Oh, don't worry about it. Let's just wait," said Magnus.

They looked out across the sky and water and along the banks.

"Is that a jar?" asked Magnus. "You see it floating in the water? It's kind of stuck in that downed branch. It's—"

"I see it, Magnus," Artemis said abruptly. "Just leave it."

"I could go get it easy enough," Magnus suggested.

"Why? No. Just leave it. Trust me."

"If you say so," said the alligator.

They waited quietly.

"I don't know what's gotten into me," Artemis sighed. "I must be—" but just then he caught sight of a cumbersome, pink bird approaching, followed by a tiny, graceful glimmer of orange.

Artemis jumped and called, "Here! Here! Over here!"

The two birds flapped and flitted in, landing on separate branches of the tree above Artemis.

"Pell! Is that you?" Artemis called.

There was a silence, and everyone waited. The delicate orange and black bird flew down to a lower branch and stared suspiciously. He looked from Artemis to Magnus and back to Artemis.

"Artie?" the bird sang.

"Yes! Pell! My stars, what are you doing here? I can't believe it!" Artemis was beside himself with excitement.

"What am *I* doing here?" Pell called indignantly, "I

always come through here. I'm on my way up north."
He laughed and twittered, "What are *you* doing here?"

"Well," Artemis began, "it's kind of a long story."

Magnus and the spoonbill nodded and looked from chipmunk to bird.

"Let me introduce you to my friends," Artemis said.

CHAPTER FOURTEEN

The Message

The chipmunk, spoonbill, and oriole sat perched on a low branch, while the alligator relaxed below. The birds were still a bit wary of the enormous reptile, but both Artemis and Magnus assured them that he would not eat them.

Artemis explained how he had ended up on the Texas coast. "I just don't understand what you're doing here," he told Pell. "Do you winter here? It's such a long way!"

"Actually, I winter in southern Mexico. I just flew six hundred miles across the Gulf without stopping.

That's the hard part."

Artemis looked confused, so Pell went on. "This is just my rest stop. There are others in my group, but I was ahead. I think they got caught in the fallout. You know, the storm. It makes travel dangerous. Hopefully they'll make it soon. Carmina will be a couple days."

Stunned, Artemis shook his head and marveled, "I had no idea you flew that far. Wow! I'm just so surprised you're here."

"You and me both!" agreed Pell.

"So…" An idea was just coming to Artemis. "You're going back to Squam Lake?"

"I sure am," said Pell. "I'm leaving tonight. I've been here two days already."

"Why so soon? Wait until tomorrow morning," pleaded Artemis.

"No. I travel at night. Not so many hawks. Less wind. Plus, it's cooler."

"But how do you know where you're going?"

"Oh, you know, the stars. I just know," replied Pell vaguely.

Seeing Artemis looking thoughtful, the bird added, "If you're thinking I can carry you, forget it. There's just no way, Artie."

"Oh, I wish! I know, but um, Pell, seriously, there is something. I need you to give my family a message."

"Okay. What should I tell them?" Pell asked.

"Please tell them that I'm alive. Tell them that I'm going to find a way to get home. Tell Ellen. Tell my parents. Please, Pell?"

"Of course, Artie. I'll tell them," Pell said quietly.

CHAPTER FIFTEEN
The Plan

Pell departed that night. Artemis felt both relief in knowing his message would reach home and sadness at losing the only connection to his past life.

"Tomorrow morning," Artemis told the spoonbill and alligator, "I'm going to make a plan."

"A plan for getting up north?" asked Flo.

"Yes," vowed Artemis.

It was quiet for a moment as they thought.

"You know," said Artemis slowly, "if those humans came down here from New Hampshire, maybe they'll be going back up there."

"Well, it stands to reason, hon," Flo agreed, surprised. "They aren't migrators though, are they?"

"No, they aren't," chimed in Magnus. "They're travelers. They usually go back to their homes. I hear them talk. Always chattering about their *own* bed. Pillow. TV. Things they must have in their homes. The way they talk, I wonder why they left in the first place. Maybe they'll head right back up there when they're done here. I hadn't thought of that, little buddy."

"Nor I, until now," marveled Artemis.

"Maybe you should go scope out their campsite and see what information you can gather," suggested Magnus.

"Are the people from New Hampshire?" asked Flo.

"I don't actually know."

"What about the car?" asked Magnus.

"What do you mean, the car?" worried Artemis.

"Well, is it a New Hampshire car?" prodded the alligator.

"How do I know? I didn't know there was a difference," moaned Artemis.

"There isn't, is there?" honked Flo.

"Well," Magnus went on, "there's usually a license

plate."

"Oh yes, I've seen those things before, hon. Some kind of identification! They're white with a bunch of dark letters and numbers!"

"If they're from Texas, that is," added Magnus.

"I'll look tomorrow," vowed Artemis. "But wait, what color should it be? I mean, if it's a New Hampshire car?"

"Hmm. Yeah," Magnus replied. "That's a good question. But it will say New Hampshire. Can you read, little buddy?"

"Not too well. Can you?" Artemis looked at them nervously.

"Good gracious, hon, not me," scoffed the spoonbill.

"I can," said Magnus. "Just look for the letters *n-e-w*. That spells 'new.' Do you know your letters?"

"Okay, yeah. I think I can recognize that," Artemis said, nodding excitedly.

"How do you know what 'new' it is, though? It could be New York or New Orleans! I've heard of those places," pointed out the bird.

"Well, it won't be New Orleans, because that's a city, not a state," corrected Magnus. "But it can give us a hint. Hopefully you won't be hitching a ride to New York. Or New Mexico. Hmm. Well, maybe we should concentrate on the Hampshire part."

After much discussion, the animals agreed it was time for bed. The spoonbill flapped away, and Magnus gave Artemis a ride back to his side of the pond.

Once settled in, Magnus mumbled, "Good night, little buddy."

"Good night, Magnus."

The two listened to the mass buzzing of the cicadas and the frequent grunts of the frogs.

Then Artemis said quietly, "They'll never believe all this. You know, if I ever get back. I'm going to miss this place."

After a pause Artemis wondered if his friend was awake.

"Well, what you need is a souvenir," reassured Magnus. He then rose and lumbered up the bank a few feet. He scratched his claw into the mud and produced a giant, yellowish tooth. "It fell out the other day. You can have it as a little remembrance of me." He grinned, displaying many more, and continued, "Don't worry. I'm fixin' to grow another."

CHAPTER SIXTEEN

Research

In the morning Artemis awoke early and whispered gently, "Magnus, I'll be back. I'm doing some research."

Magnus groaned but didn't move or say anything, so Artemis scampered away into the woods.

He remembered the way to the humans' camp. As he approached, he felt energized. Ears pricked and nose twitching, he hopped to the edge of the trees. Beyond him was the brown tent. It stood, slumped and sagging to one side, with shredded flaps in the back that billowed in the breeze. The front corner of the roof was now tied up by a rope connected to a high tree limb.

The car was parked next to the tent. Artemis stared at the back of the vehicle, looking for a license plate. He saw the small metal sign. It was white with green writing. He studied it. There was a jumble of numbers, letters, and pictures. It was too confusing.

Artemis could hear the couple talking inside the tent, so he crept closer.

"Well, I'll be glad to be back in my own bed," he heard the woman say.

"Me too," agreed the man. "I just hope we've gotten some rain up there."

"Don't worry, the yard doesn't need water yet, and

Anders is prob'ly checkin' on the house as we speak. It's Champ I'm worried about. Anders better not have let him have all those rawhide chews this time."

"You say that like he did it purposely. You know Champ just got into the bag. I'm sure Anders will be more careful."

"Maybe," she grumbled.

"Trust me, Shawna, he doesn't want to clean that up again."

Artemis heard shuffling from inside the tent, and then the voices continued. He had listened to this couple for hour after hour on the long trip down, and eventually he had tuned them out. Today was different. He listened with intensity.

"If we head out first thing tomorrow, we can get up there by Thursday," said the man.

Artemis stiffened and waited silently.

"I think so," said the woman.

There was more rustling. Artemis silently willed them to continue. "Go on," he thought. "Please. Please. Be more specific."

He heard the crackle of a plastic wrapper and smelled the salty starchy scent of human snacks. He hated how wonderful it smelled.

There was nothing but the sound of crunching and shuffling bags.

"Please. Please. Please," thought Artemis.

He waited.

Then, as if in answer to his plea, the man said, "We could stay at Squam Lake on Thursday night and then continue up to Colebrook on Friday. If we only camp one night, we could actually make it to Ben and Sylvie's wedding."

"Dale, you already replied 'no' to that," groaned the woman.

"No, I said we were a 'maybe,' and anyway they'll be…"

"What? You said we were a 'maybe?' You told me we didn't have to go! And do you really think we can get another night out of this tent?"

"We're roughin' it! Remember?" huffed the man.

"Those were your words!" she protested.

"Oh no! They were definitely yours. Roughin' it." He raised his voice in a sing-song manner and crooned, "We'll rough it, sweetie. It'll be *grrrrreat!*"

"Okay, but it might be the last time. Shoot, that invite didn't have dinner choices listed, did it? Because if it's the red snapper that Sheri had…"

Artemis had heard what he needed.

Scampering away from the camp, he cringed at the thought of riding for the next several days in the humans' hot car. This time would be different though. He would take what he needed, and he would be going home!

He just had to get himself into that car.

CHAPTER SEVENTEEN
The Concert

When Artemis raced down to the water's edge, he wasn't surprised to find Magnus still lying in his spot.

"Magnus! Magnus! They're leaving tomorrow! I heard them! I've gotta get in tomorrow!"

"Huh? Slow down."

"Okay, well, I went up there to the campsite, and I heard the humans talking," Artemis explained frantically.

"Did you check the plate?" asked Magnus.

"It doesn't matter. I heard them say it! They're going to Squam Lake, Magnus!"

"Are you sure?"

"As sure as can be. They said Squam Lake, and they would leave in the morning. So, I have to get in the car before then."

"Well, bless your fluttering little heart, little buddy," Magnus marveled.

That afternoon Magnus went out for a swim while Artemis collected nuts. When Artemis returned he was horrified to see that Magnus had one claw around the humans' glass cracker jar.

"Oh no, no, no!" worried Artemis.

"What's wrong, little buddy? You look like you ate a scoop of fire ants."

"I said to leave it!"

"Well, I did. At the time."

"Oh, Magnus, I don't know. Those crackers. They're just, well, bad luck."

"Nah. Hogwash. Anyway, I like the jar. Listen." Magnus set the jar upright in the dirt, twirled his body around, and began drumming on the lid with his tail.

"See? Isn't that a great sound?"

"Hmm," said Artemis, nervously eyeing the salty bits inside.

"How 'bout this," Magnus chuckled. "We'll feed the crumbs to those horrible fire ants." He crawled up the bank to a towering mound, opened the jar with his claws, and triumphantly flung the cracker crumbs onto the anthill. "They could use some bad luck. Look at them swarming out. Keep your distance."

Artemis stopped salivating and rubbed his scabby legs.

"Hey, little buddy, did you know that one fire ant can actually bite you, sting repeatedly, *and* send out a pheromone that calls the whole mass to attack? Did I ever tell you about my theory? Someday this continent is going to be overtaken by fire ants."

"No, Magnus. You haven't told me about that."

"Yep. That's my theory."

"Huh."

"So, we're good, right?"

"Right."

Before dusk the two friends decided that they should have a going away concert. Since Magnus didn't want an audience, it would just be the two of them.

"Aren't there usually lots of guests at a concert?" poked Artemis.

"Not mine. This is one more than usual."

"Well, all right."

Magnus collected his violin and jar and led the way to the field where they had played before.

Artemis thought about all that had happened in the last week. He was glad to be in this spot.

"It seems like ages ago that we were here," he told the alligator.

Magnus sat down and said, "Time is a funny thing. Now, we didn't do 'The Little Skunk' or 'Old Molly Hare,' did we?"

"No, but I know the skunk one! And you can teach

me the hare song!"

"Mmm," nodded the alligator as he tightened his bow.

"Really! Please teach me, teach me, Magnus!" cried Artemis.

"Calm down. I'm fixin' to do so."

Once again, they played and sang every melody they could think of. As the songs became more obscure, their words became more and more questionable.

Artemis continued to prod the grinning alligator. "Oh, oh I know, what about this one, Magnus?" Artemis jumped up and down and sang,

Twinkle twinkle little star,

How-wow wa-wa what you are

Up above the wa-wa why,

like a something in the sky,

Twinkle twinkle little star,

something something something far.

Magnus scratched out the melody on the top two strings of the violin. The open-string notes were bright and raspy, and he articulated each note with a whimsical accent. His tail kept a constant beat on the lid of his new drum.

Afterward, he put the violin down and sighed.

"Yeah, I remember that one," he chuckled, "but we used to sing it 'Tickle tickle inun dar.' I guess we didn't really think about the words."

"I guess not," Artemis laughed.

"Now for the finale, I'll play a little improvisation," announced Magnus.

He pushed the jar aside and raised his violin. With a great flourish, he drew the bow across all four strings, ending in a chord with the top two notes. He held the pitches for what seemed like an eternity, until there was no bow left, and then whipped the bow back to play a new chord with equal relish. After four chords in a row, he raised his bow, poised to continue.

Artemis inhaled and stared, wide eyed. With a great exhalation, Magnus launched into a slow and melancholy tune. His vibrato was thick and warbling. Although his smooth melody rambled, it had a sweet and mournful air. Artemis had never heard anything like it.

Just when the aching tune was becoming overwhelming, Magnus let the phrase conclude and then gracefully meandered into a contrasting jig. Suddenly the mood was light again.

Artemis began to dance and hum along with

Magnus's melody.

At the end of the song, both alligator and chipmunk contentedly ambled back down to the pond, where they spent the evening chatting and listening to the swamp sounds.

CHAPTER EIGHTEEN
A Motley Crew

It was very early when Artemis got up. He ate a quick breakfast of acorns while Magnus slept. Artemis had been saving two pecans. Instead of eating them, he decided to take them with him for Ellen. With a piece of vine, he wrapped the nuts against the giant tooth that Magnus had given him and strapped the bundle over his shoulder and around his back.

The time had come.

"Magnus," he whispered. "I have to go." His legs trembled, and his heart felt both frantic and heavy.

"I know," said the alligator with eyes still closed.

Artemis stared out at Clay Bottom Pond. The sun was just rising, and the water glimmered with gold. It was no longer the frightening mystery that it had been just a few days before. It was, in fact, quite beautiful.

"Let's go," heaved the alligator.

"You're coming too?" asked Artemis hopefully.

"Oh sure, I'll walk with you, little buddy."

As they headed up the bank, a giant flutter of pink lurched down in front of them.

"You two look like you're on a mission," honked the spoonbill.

"Oh yes, Flo! I'm so glad you're here!" cried Artemis. "Please come along with us. Today's the day."

"Were you just going to leave without saying good-bye, hon?"

"We're on a deadline here," Magnus defended. "His ride leaves this morning."

"Oh, I'm just giving y'all a hard time. Come on then. Lead the way, hon."

The odd trio crawled, hopped, and flapped through the woods.

"I know you can go faster than that," prodded the spoonbill to the alligator.

"Oh, I can, if necessary," growled Magnus.

"I think we're okay. It's barely light out," said Artemis.

Even still, Artemis scampered through the woods ahead. The large souvenir pack on his back hardly slowed him down.

Along the way, he picked up three berries and two acorns, which he stuffed into his cheeks. He would save them for the long car ride.

As he continued toward the campsite, he was startled to hear a rasping whisper from a bush just ahead of him. "Psst! Chipskunk," the voice hissed.

Artemis looked up to see Reginald, the armadillo, peering through the brush.

"Chipskunk, don't freak out," he whispered with exaggerated enunciation, "but there's an *alligator* following you."

Artemis was shocked but not because he was being followed.

"Are you blind? Even I can see him. *Get in a tree!*"

the armadillo hissed.

Reginald turned and began scurrying away.

Artemis spit out his food and called, "It's okay! He's my friend!"

The armadillo stopped and glared back in Magnus's direction.

"It appears you have many friends, hon," marveled the spoonbill.

Reginald looked bewildered but too curious to disappear entirely. Instead, he shuffled to the side of the party and watched suspiciously.

Artemis introduced his friends.

"You know, I have met one other friend," said Artemis. "Flo, I don't suppose you could go find the mother killdeer who nests on the path through that field, could you?" He pointed toward the path on which he had once traveled with the violin. "As long as you all are seeing me off, it would be nice for her to come too."

Agreeing graciously, the spoonbill flapped off. Artemis loaded his cheeks again, and the group continued their march. After distant sounds of screeching, Flo and the killdeer soon caught up to them.

"This is *ridiculous*! *Ridiculous*!" shrieked BB. "How on earth did you meet up with these creatures? *No sense*! *No sense*!"

"A little killdeer," grumbled Magnus. "Well, ain't that a fine howdy-do."

Once again, Artemis released the nuts and berries and explained his plan to the group.

CHAPTER NINETEEN
The Departure

"We'd better stop here," Artemis cautioned. "If they see all of us together, it will be, well, just weird."

The five friends peered out of the woods at the parked car. The humans were beginning to load the back.

Magnus cringed. "Looks cramped in there."

"It is," whispered Artemis.

"There's no getting me in that car, hon, but gracious me, I wouldn't mind getting a good look at some mountains."

"Shh," warned Magnus.

"In that car?" worried the killdeer. "I wouldn't go in there. I wouldn't go in there!"

"Speak for yourself, birdbrain," rasped the armadillo. "I think I'd be a good traveler. Chipskunk, maybe I should go with you and stake my claim on some new territory. Could be a fine adventure."

"Who are you calling birdbrain, hon?" huffed the spoonbill.

"Not you, Pinky. I was talking to—"

"Watch it! Watch it! It's BB! Just BB!"

"Would that be one B, two, or four? I'm going with birdbrain. BB, see? Same thing."

Artemis interrupted, "Guys, guys, guys! Be nice. Anyway, I don't think any of you have any idea how cold it gets up there. Seriously. You'd freeze on the first day of winter."

"It gets cold here too!" crackled Reginald.

"No. Not like New Hampshire. When I say freeze, I mean literally," said Artemis.

"You'd be a solid block of armadillo ice," added the spoonbill.

"That reminds me of a time," rambled Magnus, "I once did freeze solid. Two days, it was. I was right up there near the surface of the ice with my nostrils poking out. I had to just go to sleep. Frozen in a solid pond."

"Yeah, and see, you're fine. Just a little long-winded. Glad I didn't come across your creepy nostrils while walking across the ice," crackled the armadillo. "We should all get in that car. That would be one *stinky* car. Not because of me, of course."

Magnus let out a sputtering laugh. "Imagine me getting in that car too! Now that would be something! Two people, two birds, an armadillo, and an alligator. Then Artemis could get in last, and that car would burst apart just like the mitten."

"The *what*?" asked Reginald.

"You ever read *The Mitten*? No, never mind," muttered Magnus.

"It's a sweet thought, you guys," said Artemis, "but it's going to have to be just me."

"Yeah, that's for sure, little buddy," said Magnus.

Most of the boxes and bags were loaded now. The humans looked frustrated and tired, despite the fact that it was morning.

"I'll be glad to get back to New Hampshire," grumbled the man.

"You and me both! I never thought I'd miss my pillow so much," said the woman longingly.

"Geez, what a weird trip. The tent is ripped to shreds," complained the man.

Magnus whispered to Artemis, "You'd better get going, little buddy. Get your food."

"Magnus," Artemis whispered back urgently, "I'm going to miss you. You won't be lonely, will you?"

"Nah," replied the alligator. "I may be a loner, but I've never been lonely. I'll miss you, though."

Artemis felt his heart clench, and he tried to shake off his feeling of panic.

"Oh, you've got to be kidding me, Chipskunk!" Reginald huffed. "You've known him how many days? Although, who knows? Maybe that's a good chunk of your little life. What's a chipskunk's life expectancy?"

"Don't be rude, Reginald," Flo reprimanded.

"Still," tittered the killdeer, "while you guys blabber away, that car is loading up, loading up!"

"Yep," whispered Magnus. "You'll miss your ride. Take care, little buddy. Maybe we'll meet again."

"Seems unlikely, Magnus."

"Okay, go, go, go!" prodded the killdeer.

"Thanks guys," said Artemis.

The car was almost packed.

Artemis loaded his cheeks, tightened his souvenir pack, and scurried out toward the back of the car. He was just about to jump in when the woman swung around. Instead of jumping into the car, he veered away behind a log. The woman lifted the last bag and stuffed it into the back of the car.

Artemis panicked. She would see him if he approached. He had to get in!

The woman turned her back and put her hands on the hatchback door, ready to slam it shut. Artemis's legs twitched, but there was no way to jump past her without being seen.

He darted from his log and hid under the car. The

back door slammed shut. His heart pounded, and his ears began to ring.

"Let's get outta here!" called the man as he opened the driver's-side door and got in.

The woman walked around and opened the passenger-side door. Artemis scurried out from under the car and crept up behind her. He looked at the open space longingly, but she was right there in his way.

She turned slightly, looking down at the ground, and he darted back under the car. The woman climbed in, and the door slammed.

"Ugh," he groaned. "Oh, Mama, oh, Papa, oh, Ellen."

Above him, the engine started up with a roar. He crouched down in despair as the enormous vehicle passed overhead. Artemis was left in a cloud of dust.

"No, no! Ugh," he whimpered.

Desperately, he looked over at his friends. They watched in horror as the car began to drive away. The front windows went down a few inches, and then the back two followed.

Suddenly Flo honked loudly and lurched through the air. She flapped over the car, circled in front of it, and dipped down as if to crash right into the windshield.

The car skidded, and more dust rose behind it as it came to a halt. Flo hovered for a moment and then landed with a thwack directly on the front windshield of the car. As if that wasn't strange enough, she fluttered her giant pink wings impatiently and, with her enormous bill, pecked the glass three times. "Tap, tap, tap," went her beak.

The humans gasped and squealed.

This was it. Artemis would have to improvise. Pack on his back, he raced up to the car and veered around the side. With all his might, he leaped toward the back passenger-side window. As he sailed through the air, he prayed that his bulging cheeks and pack would fit. He prayed that the car would stay for one more second, and he prayed the humans wouldn't notice him.

Meanwhile, Flo perched herself on the middle of the windshield and leaned down to peer in. With bald head tilted sideways, she pressed one beady red eye up against the glass.

"Oh my!" cried the woman.

"Yow! What's that bird doin'?" gasped the man. "Just...look at that!"

Cheeks puffed out, Artemis flew straight through

the partially opened window and into the car. He gracefully landed on a box and scurried behind a familiar duffel bag.

The spoonbill pulled her head up, took one last peck for good measure, and awkwardly flapped away.

"Okay, that was just the strangest thing I've ever seen," marveled the man.

The car began to move.

Artemis settled into the fabric of the bag, spit out his nuts and berries, and breathed a sigh of relief. As the car rumbled over the dirt road, he smiled and sighed, "Anything is possible."

The End

WA

MT

OR

ID

WY

Pacific Ocean

NV

UT

CO

CA

AZ

NM

ROUTES

Artemis in the car

Pell

MEXICO

134

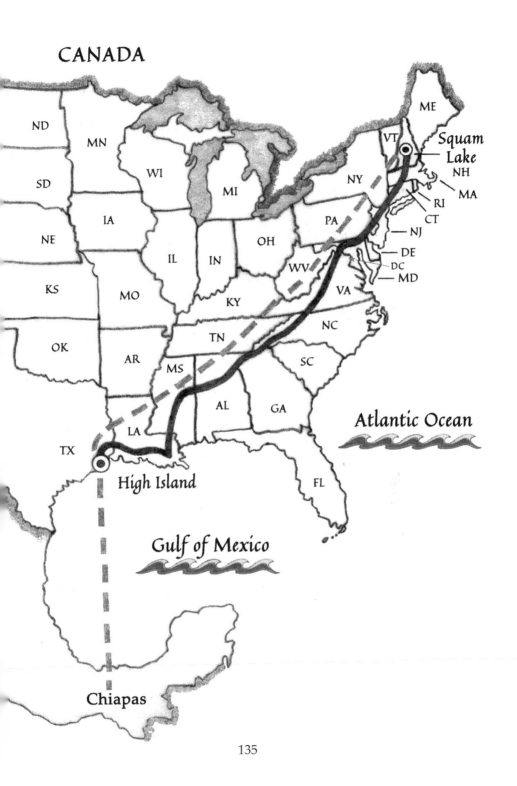

CANADA

ND

MN

SD

WI

MI

NY

ME

VT

Squam
Lake

NH

MA

RI

CT

NJ

DE

DC

MD

NE

IA

IL

IN

OH

PA

KS

MO

KY

WV

VA

OK

AR

TN

NC

MS

SC

AL

GA

Atlantic Ocean

LA

High Island

FL

Gulf of Mexico

Chiapas

135

AUTHOR

Vanessa Chase lives in Houston with her husband, daughter, and their two very bad dogs. Like Artemis, she is a transplant from New England. Despite the fact that she has lived in Texas for over twenty years, the thrill of seeing Southern wildlife has never worn off. Ms. Chase earned her graduate degree at Rice University, where she studied music. In addition to being a writer, she is a professional pianist and teaches in her Houston Heights music studio. When she is not at the piano or writing, she enjoys spending time at the beach and birding on the Bolivar Peninsula.

I would like to thank ecotour guide and naturalist Glenn Olsen, who introduced me to the world of bird watching and verified my scientific facts. Thanks to my fabulous illustrator Jo Gershman for breathing life into my characters and keeping me on track throughout the production of the book. I am grateful to all my dear friends who have proofread and encouraged me along the way. I am especially grateful to my husband and daughter for welcoming Artemis and his animal friends into our daily lives, and for entertaining my endless discussions of commas, apostrophes, alligators, and armadillos. And finally, I would like to thank my faithful mom and dad. Without their unwavering encouragement and support, I would never have started, let alone finished the book.

ILLUSTRATOR

Jo Gershman lives in Seattle with her husband and two very opinionated cats. Her illustrations appear in over 35 books for children and adults, including *Jilly's Terrible Temper Tantrums & How She Outgrew Them*, *The Land of Walloo*, *The Nutcracker Ballet*, and the *WindDancers*® Series. Her watercolors and illuminated manuscripts are in private collections around the world and her work can be seen at www.jogershman.com.

Thank you Painters of Bumping Lake as always for your sharp eyes and detailed critiques. Thank you Martin for your calm, talent, and technical expertise. And thank you to my husband Daniel for tolerating the long hours with unfailing support, understanding, and chocolate.

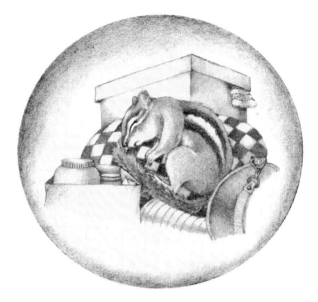

visit Artemis at

www.ScreechOwlPress.com

Made in the USA
Columbia, SC
10 March 2018